My mob going to the beach

Published by Black Ink Press 2004, reprinted 2008, 2010 and 2011

Yalga-binbi Institute for Community Development
PO Box 217 Thuringowa, Queensland 4817
07 4773 5077

Printed by GEON

DEDICATION

SE: for my family

JE: for Pat Cornford at the MRC

CiP data
Emmerton, Sylvia (1953-2005). My mob going to the beach.
For children.
ISBN 978-1-86334-014-4
1. Families, Aboriginal Australian - Juvenile fiction.
2. Beaches - Australia - Juvenile fiction.
I. Elliott, Jaquanna. II. Title.
A823.4

Australia Council for the Arts

My mob going to the beach

written by Sylvia Emmerton
illustrated by Jaquanna Elliott

BLACK INK PRESS

One day the grown-ups said we were going to the beach.

We would take some blankets, a couple of billies and some tea and sugar.

We were going to sleep there too. Just for one night though.

We didn't have a car so we would have to walk.

We started out early and soon came to some cattle yards. We had to cross a yard where there was a huge bull in one corner.

The grown-ups and the big kids walked across quietly.

But not us.

We ran as fast as we could.

Shortly after that we came to a camp near a billabong. We knew the people in the camp so we stopped for a visit.

The grown-ups and the big kids sat down for a yarn.

But not us.

We went looking for wild duck eggs
in the grass beside the billabong.

We started out again and had to cross through the cemetery. It was getting very hot. The grown-ups and the big kids stopped at the taps for a drink.

But not us.

Promoted to

We sat under the taps
and got wet all over.

Finally we got to the beach. We found a big shady tree to make our camp.

The tide was out so we went searching through the rocks and pools. The grown-ups and the big kids searched for oysters. Yuk!

But not us.

We went looking for cockles. Yum!

The grown ups made a fire on the beach and we cooked the cockles and some oysters in the coals.

When we finished our feed, the tide had come in. The grown-ups and the big kids went fishing and crabbing.

But not us.

We went swimming and
played in the sand.

Late in the afternoon, we cooked the fish and crabs and had a big feed.

It started to get dark and the grown-ups and the big kids sat around the campfire to yarn and tell stories.

But not us.

We fell
fast asleep.

Sylvia Emmerton of Kalkadoon descent was born in Townsville, living in the suburbs of Garbutt and Currajong until she was six. This story is a compilation of memories from those years in the fifties.

Her family moved away for a long time and they moved around frequently. As an adult with her own children she came back to Townsville to attend University for four years and then to teach for ten years.

This story won a Black Ink award in 2002 and is Sylvia's first published book.

Jaquanna Elliott was born in Dubbo and raised in Adelaide, Sydney and the desert regions of South Australia. She is a descendant of the Dunghutti people of the NSW north coast.

She has lived in Townsville for 13 years and in 1999 took up painting and sculpture. She resides with her daughter Angie and cat Sylvester.

Jaquanna has used gouache (water based paint) on paper to do these illustrations. This is her first picture story book.

Black Ink is a community-based Indigenous writing, illustrating and publishing project based in North Queensland, part of Yalga-binbi Institute for Community Development. This is the fourth book published.

Black Ink supports writers and illustrators, editors and designers all over Australia who are interested in providing good books for Indigenous children and youth.

We will publish in all Indigenous languages and a variety of media.

Black Ink ensures that individual artist copyright and community interests are both respected.

Black Ink

N
NW
NE
W
E
SW
SE
S
MAGNETIC ISLAND
ROWES BAY
CAMP
CEMETERY
AIRPORT
BILLABONG
HAPPY VALLEY
CATTLE YARDS
GARBUTT